FAVORITE
Dog BREEDS

GERMAN SHEPHERDS

by Martha E. H. Rustad

AMICUS HIGH INTEREST • AMICUS INK

Amicus High Interest and Amicus Ink are imprints of Amicus
P.O. Box 1329, Mankato, MN 56002
www.amicuspublishing.us

Copyright © 2018 Amicus. International copyright reserved in all countries. No part of this book may be reproduced in any form without written permission from the publisher.

Library of Congress Cataloging-in-Publication Data
Names: Rustad, Martha E. H. (Martha Elizabeth Hillman), 1975- author.
Title: German shepherds / by Martha E. H. Rustad.
Description: Mankato, Minnesota : Amicus High Interest, Amicus Ink, [2018] | Series: Favorite dog breeds | Audience: Ages 5-9. | Audience: K to grade 3. | Includes bibliographical references and index.
Identifiers: LCCN 2016033326 (print) | LCCN 2016038408 (ebook) | ISBN 9781681511276 (library binding) | ISBN 9781681521589 (pbk.) | ISBN 9781681512174 (ebook) | ISBN 9781681512174 (pdf)
Subjects: LCSH: German shepherd dog--Juvenile literature. | Dog breeds--Juvenile literature.
Classification: LCC SF429.G37 R87 2018 (print) | LCC SF429.G37 (ebook) | DDC 636.737/6--dc23
LC record available at https://lccn.loc.gov/2016033326

Photo Credits: GlobalP/iStock cover; Eric Isselee/Shutterstock 2, 8-9; Nancy Nehring/iStock 5; ullstein bild/ullstein bild/Getty Images 6-7; Aleksandra Dabrowa/Shutterstock 10-11; U.S. Army/Visual Information Specialist Pierre-Etienne Courtejoie/WikiCommons 13; Ershova_Veronika/iStock 14-15; squiremi/iStock 17; Best dog photo/Shutterstock 18; Stone36/Shutterstock 20-21; rtem/Shutterstock 22

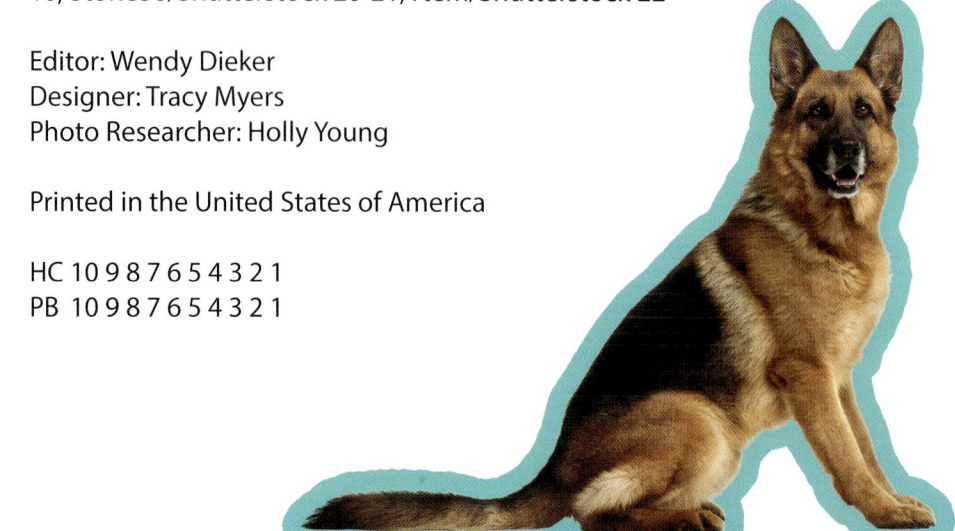

Editor: Wendy Dieker
Designer: Tracy Myers
Photo Researcher: Holly Young

Printed in the United States of America

HC 10 9 8 7 6 5 4 3 2 1
PB 10 9 8 7 6 5 4 3 2 1

TABLE OF CONTENTS

Police Dog	4
Sheep Herders	7
Thick Coat	8
Long Muzzle	11
Working Dogs	12
Dog Athletes	15
Puppies	16
A Loud Bark	19
Friend for Life	20
How Do You Know	
It's a German Shepherd?	22
Words to Know	23
Learn More	24
Index	24

POLICE DOG

A dog stands next to a police officer. The officer tells her to find something. The dog obeys. She sniffs. She finds it. This is a German shepherd. They are smart, **loyal** dogs.

5

6

SHEEP HERDERS

The German shepherd **breed** started in Germany. They kept flocks of sheep safe. Today German shepherds still work hard. Many help as **guide dogs**.

Furry Fact
German shepherd dogs can learn to climb ladders. They can even learn to open doors.

THICK COAT

German shepherds have thick fur. A **double coat** keeps them warm. Their fur sheds a lot. It is most often black and tan. Some dogs have reddish or gray coats.

Furry Fact
A few German shepherds have white fur. Some people think this is a different breed.

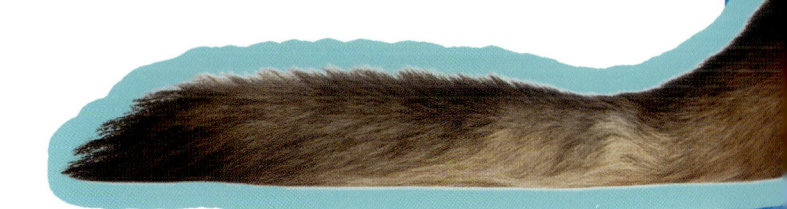

9

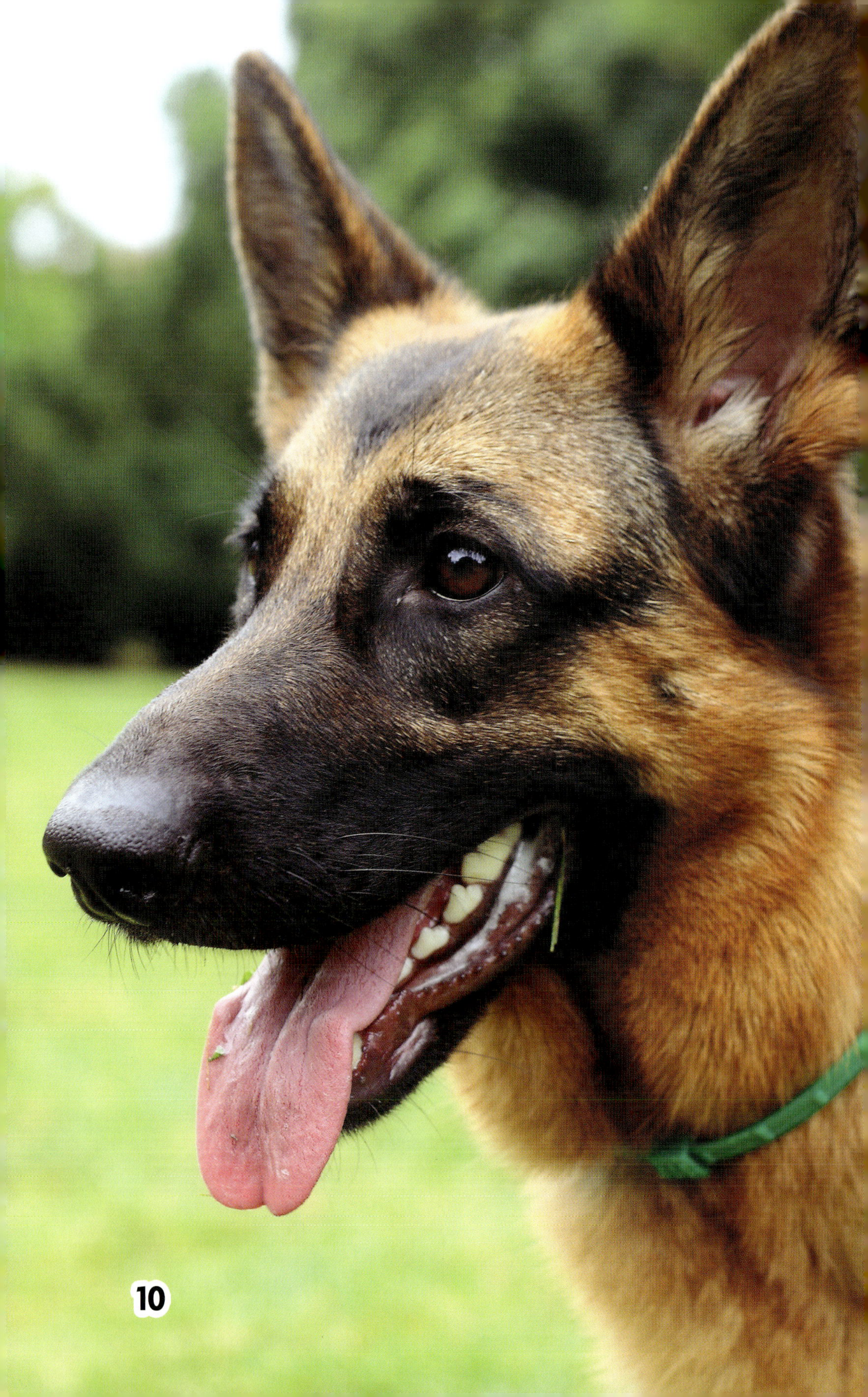

LONG MUZZLE

A **muzzle** is a dog's nose and mouth. German shepherds have a long muzzle. Their strong jaws can bite hard. They also have a strong sense of smell. Their noses track many scents.

Furry Fact
A German shepherd's bite is almost as strong as a wolf's bite.

WORKING DOGS

German shepherds seem to enjoy working. They have a lot of energy. These dogs learn quickly. Many German shepherds work in the military. They sniff for bombs.

13

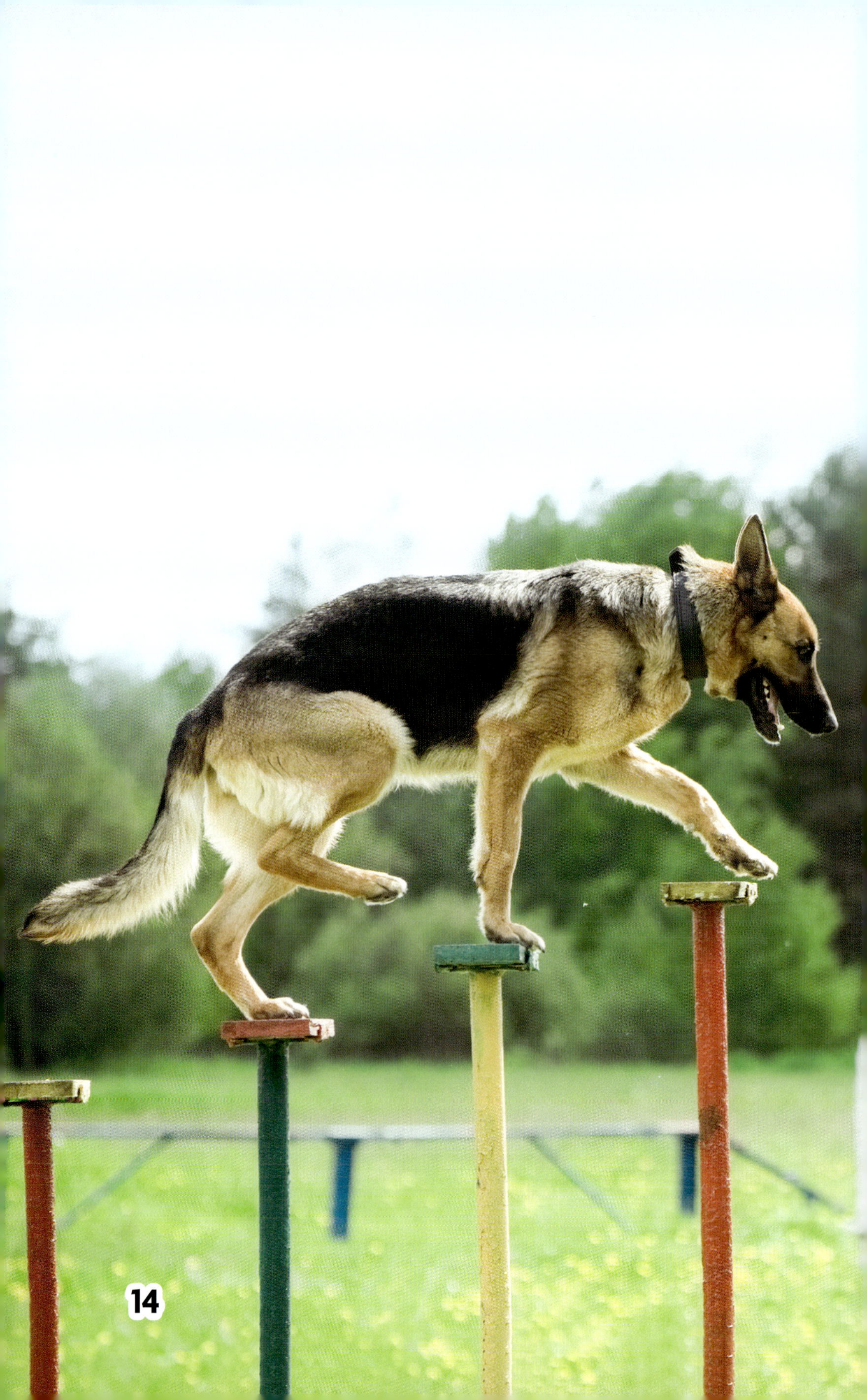

DOG ATHLETES

German shepherds are dog athletes. They are strong. They run fast. These dogs are good at **agility contests**. They can race through hard courses. They crawl and jump. Hoops and ramps are no problem.

PUPPIES

Up to ten puppies are born in a **litter**. Newborn German shepherds have floppy ears. Their ears point up after six months. Puppies are playful. They like to pounce and play catch.

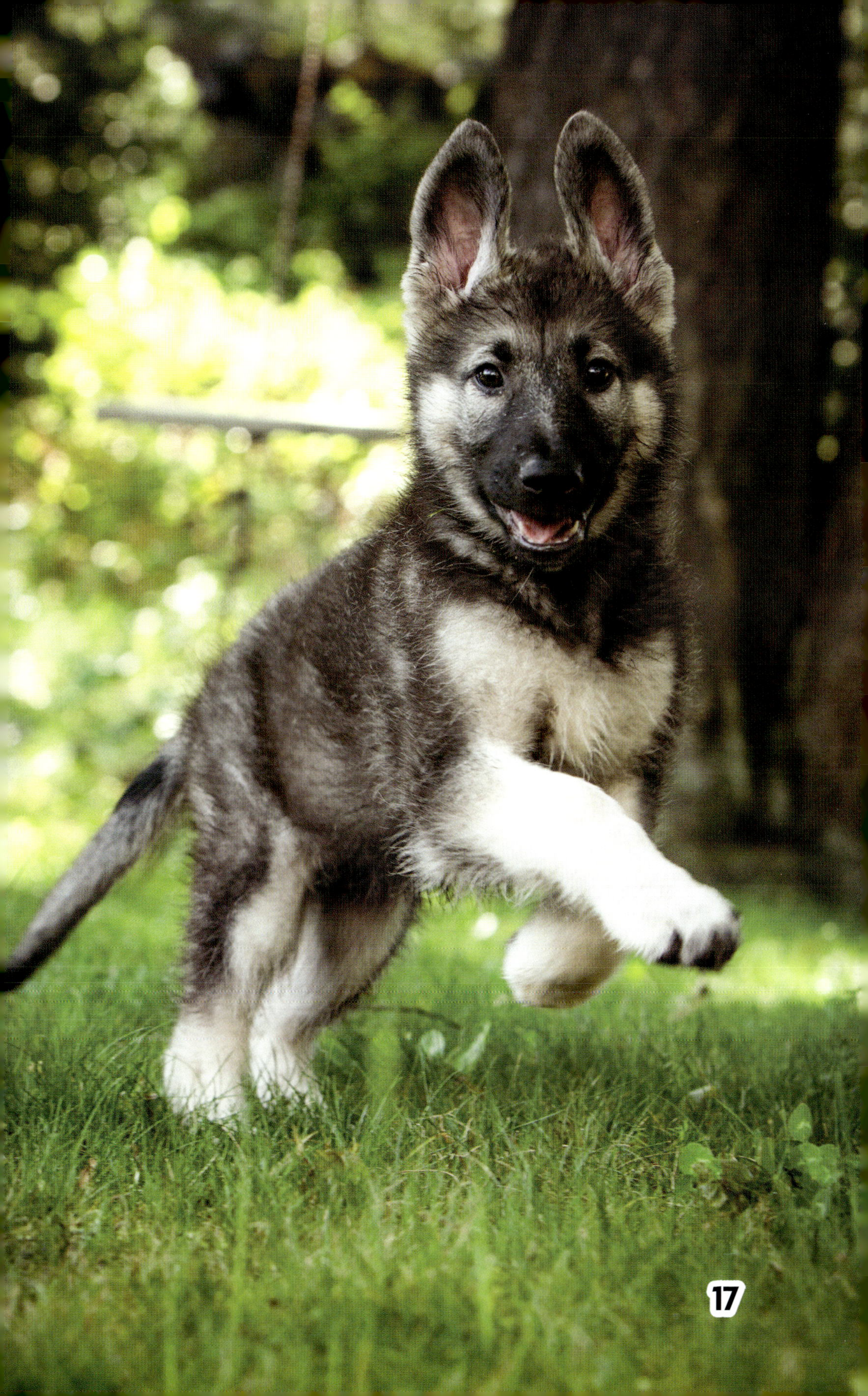

18

A LOUD BARK

German shepherds bark loudly. A bark is a warning. They alert owners of strangers. This breed makes a good guard dog. Bark!

FRIEND FOR LIFE

German shepherds do not like to be alone. They like to be with their owners. A German shepherd will be a loyal friend for life.

Furry Fact
A German shepherd is often strongly loyal to only one person in the family.

HOW DO YOU KNOW IT'S A GERMAN SHEPHERD?

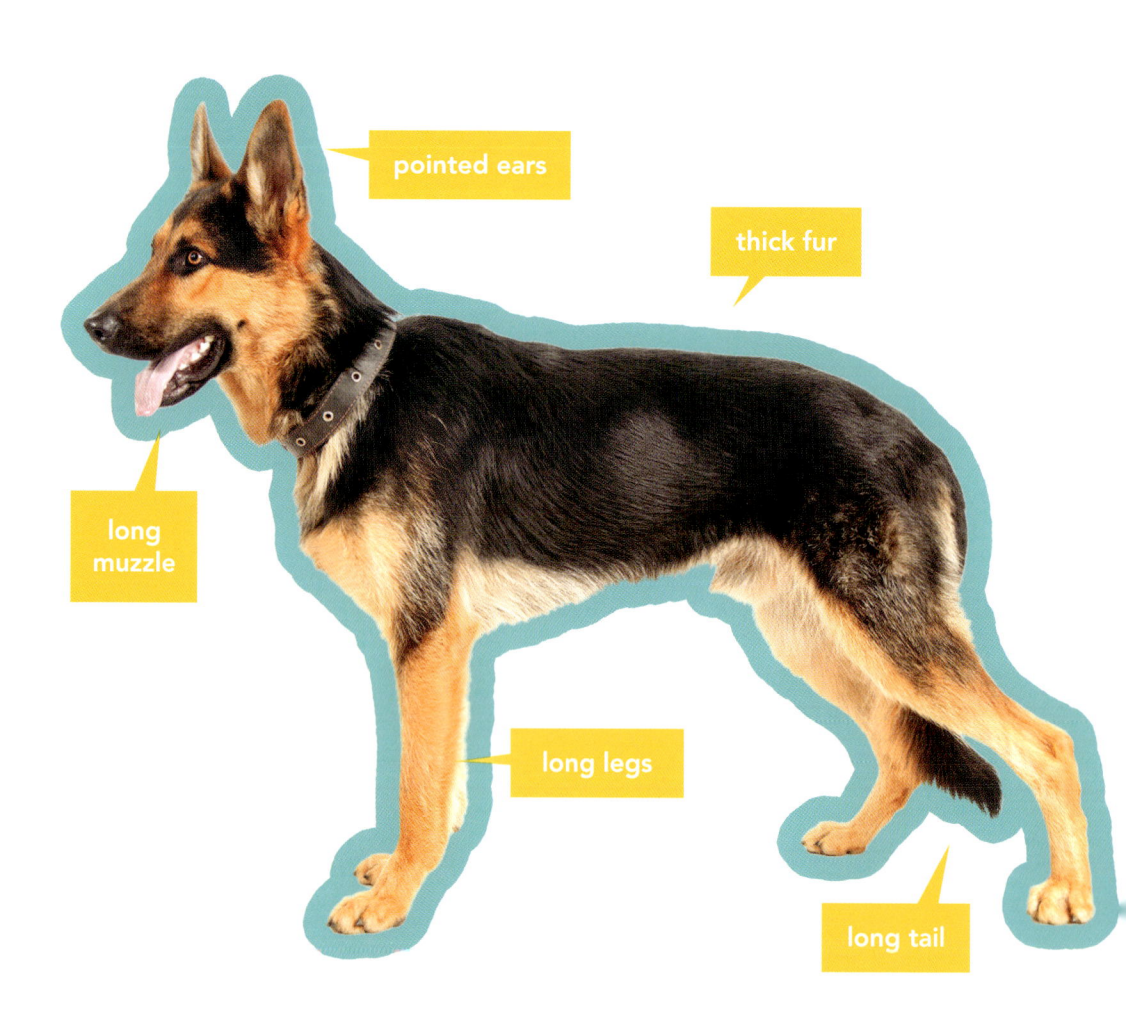

pointed ears

thick fur

long muzzle

long legs

long tail

WORDS TO KNOW

agility contest – a contest where dogs run an obstacle course of ramps, tunnels, and hoops as fast as they can

breed – a dog that has certain features that make it different from other kinds of dogs

double coat – a coat of fur with two layers

guide dog – a dog trained to lead a person who can't see well

litter – a group of puppies born at the same time

loyal – to love and be faithful to someone

muzzle – the nose and mouth of a dog

LEARN MORE

Books
Barnes, Nico. *German Shepherds.* Minneapolis: Abdo Kids, 2015.

Bowman, Chris. *German Shepherds.* Blastoff! Readers: Awesome Dogs. Minneapolis: Bellwether Media, 2016.

Websites
American Kennel Club: German Shepherd
http://www.akc.org/dog-breeds/german-shepherd-dog/

Animal Planet: German Shepherd
http://www.animalplanet.com/tv-shows/dogs-101/videos/german-shepherd/

FBI: About Our Dogs
https://www.fbi.gov/fun-games/kids/kids-dogs

INDEX

agility contests 15

barking 19

fur 8

history 7

loyalty 4, 20

muzzle 11

police 4

puppies 16

working 4, 7, 12

Every effort has been made to ensure that these websites are appropriate for children. However, because of the nature of the Internet, it is impossible to guarantee that these sites will remain active indefinitely or that their contents will not be altered.